W.i.t.c.h.

Will   Irma   Taranee   Cornelia   Hay Lin

ADVENTURES

Stolen Spring

© 2005 Disney Enterprises, Inc.
Text copyright © 2002 by Lene Kaaberbol
W.I.T.C.H. Will Irma Taranee Cornelia Hay Lin
is a trademark of Disney Enterprises, Inc.
Volo® is a registered trademark of Disney Enterprises, Inc.
Volo/Hyperion Books for Children are imprints of
Disney Children's Book Group, L.L.C.

Printed in Singapore
First U.S. edition
1 3 5 7 9 10 8 6 4 2

This book is set in 11.5/16 Hiroshige Book.
ISBN 0-7868-0980-9
Visit www.clubwitch.com

W.i.t.c.h.

Will   Irma   Taranee   Cornelia   Hay Lin

ADVENTURES

Stolen Spring

By Lene Kaaberbol

VOLO

an imprint of
HYPERION BOOKS FOR CHILDREN
New York

Once, long ago, when the universe was young, spirits and creatures lived under the same sky. There was only one world, only one vast realm, governed by the harmonies of nature. But evil entered the world, and found its place in the hearts and minds of spirits and creatures alike, and the world shattered into many fragments. The realm was split between those who wished for peace and those who lived to gain power over others and cause them pain. To guard and protect what was good in the worlds, the mighty stronghold of Candracar was raised in the middle of infinity.

There, a congregation of powerful spirits and creatures keep vigilance; chief among them is the Oracle. His wisdom is much needed; at times,

Candracar is all that keeps evil from entering where it should have no place.

There is also the Veil. A precious barrier between good and evil, guarded by unlikely girls.

Irma has power over water. Taranee can control fire. Cornelia has all the powers of earth. Hay Lin holds the lightness and the freedom of air. And Will, the Keeper of the Heart of Candracar, holds a powerful amulet in which all of the natural elements meet to become energy, pure and strong.

Together they are W.I.T.C.H.—five Guardians of the Veil. And the universe needs them. . . .

1

"You're hurting the flowers," said Lilian accusingly. "Mom says we're not supposed to touch her plants."

I sighed. My little sister Lilian was annoying me again. As usual.

"I'm just picking off the dead flowers," I said. "You're *supposed* to do that. It's called pruning a plant." Carefully, I pinched another wilted hibiscus flower off the stem.

With a loud crack, the pot suddenly split in two, and potting soil spilled onto the living-room floor. Startled, I let go of the hibiscus.

"You broke it," cried Lilian. "Mom! Cornelia broke the plant!"

"Hush!" I hissed. "Be quiet, or I'll . . ."

But it was too late.

"Cornelia!" my mother yelled.

Mom was in the doorway, glaring at me. "I've *told* you not to fool around with my plants. How could you be so careless?"

"But I didn't do anything!" I said.

"Oh, really?" my mom said. "And I guess you want me to believe that the little plant just all of a sudden decided to break its pot all by itself?"

I scowled at the plant. It didn't look little. As a matter of fact, it looked quite large. The plant was practically growing as I watched.

Wait a second. Growing as I watched?

A suspicion sprouted in my mind. I looked at my hands. No, I didn't have a green thumb. But I did have power over the earth. I knew I could make things grow when I wanted to. Only, this time, I hadn't wanted to. I hadn't tried to make *anything* happen. And the plant still had a major growth spurt that had split the pot. What was going on?

"Well, don't just stand there," my mom scolded. "Get a new pot for the plant."

"Cornelia was punching it," said Lilian self-importantly.

"*Pruning*, you pest!" I hissed.

"Don't talk to your sister like that, Cornelia," my mother said. "Go get another pot, and while you're at it, get the vacuum cleaner, and take care of this mess that you made."

"I didn't do anything!" I protested again. "Honestly, sometimes you'd think slavery hadn't been abolished. . . ."

"Cornelia," my mother said with a stern look. "You're *this* close to being grounded!"

I shut my mouth. She wouldn't do that, would she? Not with Hay Lin's show coming up. I shot a sideways glance at her.

"Well?" Mom was still glaring at me.

I decided not to risk it.

"All right, all right," I said.

By the time I was done repotting the plant and cleaning up the mess, I was very late. I rushed off to Sheffield Institute. Normally, I don't go to school on Saturdays, but I had a dress rehearsal for Hay Lin's fashion show.

When I got to school, Irma came running up to me. She almost knocked me down with the load of boxes she was carrying.

"You're late!" she snapped at me.

"Sorry," I said. I was in no mood to get into details—especially with Irma, the unofficial queen of tardiness.

"Hey, watch out!" Will called as she tried to maneuver down the hallway with a large ladder. "You're so late!"

Couldn't a girl be late every once in a while?

I walked past Will and straight in to school. I found Taranee mounting a camera on a tripod. Peering at her light meter, she moved back suddenly, stepping firmly on my right foot.

"Oh, er, sorry," she muttered. "I *wish* Will would light the stage better. This isn't the best light for photos." Then Taranee seemed to focus on me. "Oh, Hay Lin is looking for you. You're late, aren't you?"

"Yes," I hissed, and limped into the classroom that had been converted into a dressing room. A bunch of brightly colored skirts and dresses were scattered all over the room. In the middle of the room Hay Lin was standing with a frown on her face.

"No, not that one!" she said to a girl named Kara. "That's for the finale. Where is . . ." she continued, and then she noticed me standing there. "Oh, there you are. You're . . ."

"Late." I said, finishing her sentence. "Yes. I know. Sorry."

Hay Lin put her hands together and smiled at me. "I was about to say, you're a very welcome sight. *Please* help us get this mess straightened out."

I sighed. All the irritation of the morning flew

out of me. I smiled warmly at Hay Lin.

"I'd be glad to," I said.

I wanted this fashion show to be a success. Hay Lin had worked like a crazy person to get all the dresses finished in time, and she really, really deserved a good show.

Helping out with Hay Lin's fashion show was one of those situations when it was nice to be ordinary. I don't mean boring-ordinary, I just mean not magical. This show used lots of our energy, but not an ounce of Guardian magic. I loved discussing the music, the hairstyles, the clothes, and the costume changes, instead of having our lives threatened by eight-foot-tall monsters with reptilian tails. It felt like a nice break.

Don't get me wrong. Being part of W.I.T.C.H. was one of the most exciting and important things that had ever happened in my life. When I first discovered what I could do with my powers, I was both proud and a little scared. And then, when Will got the Heart of Candracar, we found out that we were all linked through the Heart.

It turns out that each of us—Will, Irma, Taranee, Hay Lin, and I—has power over one of the natural elements. Mine is earth, of course, and Hay Lin has awesome powers over air. Taranee can play with fire, and Irma can do the most amazing things with water. And because Will unites us all with her power to control pure energy, she is our leader.

In the beginning, it was a little hard for me to accept being a Guardian. I mean, I've always been an I'll-believe-it-when-I-see-it kind of person. Both my feet were always firmly on the ground, which I suppose is appropriate for an earth girl. And yet, there we were, the five of us, sharing the same strange dreams, and with all these magical powers at our fingertips.

On top of everything else, we discovered that not everyone was thrilled that Candracar had anointed five new Guardians. We had enemies in worlds we had never even heard of. Later, I found out we also had friends. Very good friends, but that's a whole other story. I have to admit, it was all a little overwhelming—a sort of dream come true *and* nightmare all rolled into one. So sometimes it felt good to do stuff that had nothing to do with saving the world, stuff that just let you be fourteen and completely unmagical.

Or so I thought. But that day, unbeknownst to me, magic was already at work in Heatherfield. And it was a type of magic that would soon become very hard to ignore.

"Ladies and gentlemen, the Sheffield Institute is proud to present Spring Fashions by our very own Hay Lin!" announced the show's emcee.

"Wow! There are so many people," whispered Taranee, standing next to me in the wings of the auditorium stage. "I'm glad it's you who's going out there, and not me!"

"You could do it," I said with a smile.

"No, I couldn't," Taranee whispered. "You look so beautiful and calm."

I wasn't feeling completely calm. My hands were damp, and I kept wanting to run back to the dressing room. I once read an interview of a supermodel in some fashion magazine. "The trick is to go out there on the catwalk *knowing* you are beautiful," the model had said. "Then the audience will believe it, too." Easy for her to say. I touched my hair nervously.

The music began. It was my cue. Hay Lin had picked a song by our favorite band, Karmilla.

"Go!" said Taranee, giving me a slight push toward the stage.

I willed my feet to move. With a smile that felt plastered to my face, I stepped out onto the runway. Somewhere behind me, Hay Lin was probably biting her nails and having a mini–panic attack. I know I would have been. If the clothes that I had designed were being shown, I'd be a total wreck! But they'd like them, wouldn't they? They had to admire the cool style, or they obviously had *no* taste!

I heard catcalls from the back of the auditorium. I knew right away it was Uriah and his goofy gang of friends. There was no way I was going to let them ruin Hay Lin's big night! I kept on walking, with my runway smile.

I found I was moving down the aisle with fierce determination. Look at *this*, I thought. This is a great dress.

I turned so that the turquoise skirt flared around my knees. I shot a look over my shoulder, mostly to keep the boys quiet, and strutted across the stage.

As I walked back into the wings, Irma walked out wearing another one of Hay Lin's creations. She gave me a quick, startled look. Why? Was something wrong? I quickly checked to see if I had ripped anything or popped a button, but everything looked okay.

"Wow!" said Taranee when she saw me, with the same startled look on her face. "You looked *fierce* out there."

"I was just trying to keep Uriah and his goons quiet," I muttered. "Here, can you help me with the back zipper? I can't get to it."

"Well, you certainly made people look at you!" Taranee said. "And I got a really great picture."

I stepped out of the turquoise dress and into a red one decorated with the beads that were part of Hay Lin's unique style. Hay Lin was making frantic hand gestures for me to hurry up. I started up the stairs.

"Shoes!" Taranee whispered. "You need to change shoes!"

Whoops. No, the turquoise sandals certainly *didn't* go with the red dress. Talk about a close call! I had almost made a major fashion faux pas. Quickly I kicked them off and, hopping from one foot to the other, put on the scarlet ones that Taranee had handed me. I had a second to calm myself; I took a deep breath, and it was time to hit the stage again.

"What's that in your hair?" asked Hay Lin as I passed her.

What? I mouthed.

"There, that green thing . . . no, never mind, you're on!" she said, pushing me.

Green? I had no time to check.

I had seen fashion shows. But until I was actually in one, I hadn't realized just how crazy it was behind the scenes for the models. How did they manage to look so calm?

The show went by in a blur of zipping and unzipping, rapid mirror checks, musical cues, and applause. People clapped every time a new dress appeared. And though Hay Lin still looked superbusy, her smile had grown into a huge, happy grin.

When it was time for the finale, all of the models walked onstage wearing different white dresses and holding pink flowers. Hay Lin stood at center stage, beaming like a small sun, bowing to the cheering audience. I even noticed Uriah and his gang clapping. Of course, that might have had something to do with Mrs. Knickerbocker, our principal, standing right behind them.

That was when it happened. Out of the corner of my eye, I saw a green flash. And then the pink flowers in my hands burst into full bloom.

The crowd went, "Oh!" and then began to clap even more fiercely.

"Great effect!" someone called out.

I just stared at the flower, wanting to get rid of it, throw it away. First my mother's hibiscus, now this. What was going on?

Behind us, the lights dimmed, and some people began to leave, while others drifted backstage to congratulate Hay Lin and the "models."

"Thanks, Cornelia," said Hay Lin, giving me a hug. "Thanks for all your help. And for the special effect . . . Nice springtime touch, earth girl," she whispered, grinning.

"But I didn't mean to do anything. . . ." I said.

And I hadn't. That should have been my first clue that something was wrong. Unfortunately, in all the craziness of the after-show, the little burst of green totally slipped my mind. Looking back, I can't imagine how I could have been so unaware. Something strange was definitely going on—and it revolved around me.

2

"Cornelia, wake *up!*" Lilian said, bouncing up and down on my bed like a maniac.

"Go away," I snapped hoarsely and swatted at her with one hand. "Get out!"

"You're in the paper," she said.

"Look, just get lost, or . . . what?" I tried to focus on what she had just said. "What did you say?"

"Your picture's in the paper," Lilian replied. She ran out of the room chanting, "Cornelia's in the paper! Cornelia's in the paper!"

I stumbled out of bed and quickly ran downstairs. I half expected my parents to be anxiously awaiting my appearance. I was wrong.

In the kitchen, Dad was calmly having his breakfast and skimming through the newspaper.

"Hi, sweetie. Nice picture," he said.

"Let me see!" I said, looking at the table where the paper was spread out.

He pushed the paper toward me. And there it was. SHEFFIELD SETS THE FASHION, the caption said, and underneath was a large color photo of me glaring over my shoulder. It was obviously the moment that I had stared Uriah down. Except that in the picture I looked more intense than angry and the turquoise dress made my eyes seem unbelievably blue.

"I . . . I look just like a real model," I said.

My dad smiled at me. "You're definitely a picture," he said. "You always are."

"No, I mean, I look . . . I look *good*." It was like a real glamour shot. Normally, when I look in the mirror, I see hair that I wish had a bit more curl to it, a nose that's a little too narrow. But this picture showed something completely different from that.

"Your friend Taranee took it," he said.

The words PHOTO: TARANEE COOK were printed in the corner. The article was supercomplimentary. It talked about the fashion show and about Hay Lin, and there was a short comment from Mrs. Knickerbocker about how "we always encourage creative tendencies in our students."

"I've got to call the others," I said, "and make

sure they've all seen this. I can't believe it!"

And that was when I noticed another story on the page.

RECORD-BREAKING BEECH TREE

YESTERDAY A GIANT TREE IN HANABAKER PARK, KNOWN AS THE HANABAKER BEECH, WAS FULL OF NEW SPRING LEAVES—A MONTH AHEAD OF SCHEDULE. "I'VE NEVER SEEN ANYTHING LIKE IT," SAID CHIEF OF STAFF THOMAS GREENBOW, "AND I'VE WORKED IN THIS PARK FOR ALMOST THIRTY YEARS." METEOROLOGISTS SAY THAT TEMPERATURES "HAVE NOT BEEN ABOVE AVER-AGE," BUT OTHER UNSEASONAL GROWTH SPURTS AROUND THE PARK ATTEST TO THE FACT THAT SPRINGTIME HAS DEFINITELY ARRIVED—EARLY!

It was probably coincidental and probably meant nothing. But I still had a nagging feeling that something was up. I couldn't help remembering the flowers from the show that had suddenly bloomed. And yesterday, on my way to the dress rehearsal, I had passed through Hanabaker Park and right by that very tree. The story did seem strange. And I was starting to feel strange, too!

"I never thought *I'd* be saying this to *you*," said Irma. "But seriously, Cornelia, I think you're just imagining things. It's spring. Trees get leaves in the spring."

"Not this early, they don't!" I couldn't help raising my voice. My friends thought I was making things up. It was beginning to make me want to scream—even though we were in the middle of the school cafeteria.

"Oh," Irma said, giving me a look. "So, naturally, this new growth must have something to do with you?"

"It could be global warming," said Taranee, trying to calm me down.

"It hasn't been particularly hot," I replied.

"But can't you feel whether you do something magical?" Will asked, taking a bite of her sandwich. "Personally, I don't think I've done any unintentional magic since . . . well, not for a long time, anyway."

"What else could it be?" I asked, looking around the table.

Our heads were all close together and we had formed a little wall because this was *not* the kind of discussion we wanted to share with the whole world, or, in this case, the entire Sheffield Institute cafeteria. Luckily, as members of W.I.T.C.H., we were pretty good at the whole thing. So it was quite a shock when a photographer's flash suddenly went off in our faces. Startled, I looked up and ended up catching the next flash right in my eyes.

"Hey, stop that. . . ." I began.

"Oooooh, pleeeease, Ms. Hale, just one more, come on, give us the famous smile. . . ."

Even though I could barely see between all the spots dancing in front of my eyes, I still recognized Uriah's ugly face.

"Get lost, Uriah!" I snapped angrily. Uriah was always showing up where he was least wanted.

He kept on jumping around and taking pictures like he was a member of the paparazzi.

"Look this way, Ms. Hot Supermodel," Uriah yelled. "Work it. Wonderful . . ."

I noticed that people were actually laughing. It was ridiculous. I felt like making Uriah swallow his camera. It would serve him right. But I managed to control myself and, instead, gave him my sweetest smile.

"Very funny, Uriah," I said. "Here's a question. Did you just buy that camera?"

He looked slightly surprised by my calm

response, as if I weren't following the script he'd had in mind.

"Yeah," he said. "It's new. Why?"

"Well, I hope they gave you the *fool*proof kind," I said with a straight face.

It wasn't much of a joke, but it was enough to make most of the cafeteria audience laugh *at* Uriah instead of *with* him.

"Ha-ha," he said, and turned around and stalked sulkily out of the cafeteria.

The bell rang, and we all rushed to class. I was thinking about Taranee's suggestion of global warming for the rest of the day. I was still considering the prospect of the earth's warming when I walked out of school. A bright flash interrupted my thoughts. I was blinded by a photographer's flash *again*.

"Uriah!" I snapped. "*Once* is funny, twice is just plain—"

And then I stopped, realizing that Uriah wasn't the one taking the pictures.

"Ms. Hale?" said the stranger waiting outside the classroom. "Just one more picture, please. And then I'd like to talk to you for a moment, if that's all right with you."

"Me? What about?" I said, startled. Who was this guy? He looked a little too perfect to be from

Heatherfield. He was a little too tan, a little too tidy, with an expensive-looking haircut and a cinnamon-colored shirt that matched his eyes. His shoes were brown, too, I noticed, and he had on crisp white linen pants. Overall, he was very well put together.

"My name is A. C. Jones," he said, holding out a hand. "Just call me Acey; most people do. I am personal assistant to Tony Sacharino, the fashion designer. And today is your lucky day!" He smiled and gave her a wink. "Mr. Sacharino saw your picture in yesterday's paper," he continued, "and you really caught his eye. He thought you really grabbed the camera's attention. Have you done any professional modeling? Fashion photography, I mean?"

"No," I said. There were kids rushing by trying to get to class. His next words caught me totally off guard.

"Well," he said, smiling brilliantly, "would you like to?"

€ € ▲ ◉ €

"The line of clothing is called Fairy-Tale Fantasies," I said excitedly. I was trying to remain cool, but it was impossible. "And *Red Hot* is doing six whole pages on them, and they want *me* to be in the shoot. Please, please, please,

Mom . . . can I do it? They'll even pay me."

"Cornelia, honey . . ." my mom began hesitantly.

I didn't give her a chance to finish. "It'll only take two days, and it's nearby. Right outside Heatherfield, actually, at Ladyhold—you know that really beautiful house that looks like a castle? And Acey said I could bring a few friends, as long as they didn't get in the way. Just think how exciting it would be for Hay Lin to watch a professional designer at work. . . ."

My mom did not look thrilled. "Cornelia," she said, "you're only fourteen."

I held back a groan. Here we go again, I thought.

"But Mom, it would be so much fun!" I begged.

"Will it really make you happy to stand in front of a camera for two days and do nothing but smile?" Mom asked in a concerned tone. "Or pout, or whatever it is that models are supposed to do these days . . ." Her voice trailed off.

"Modeling Hay Lin's dresses was amazing," I explained. "And this would be . . . this would be even more amazing because it's *real*. I'd be a real model, and everybody reads *Red Hot*, even you, Mom. . . ."

"Even me?" she said slyly, and I noticed a glint in her eyes that I hoped was humor. "Are you implying that I'm too *old* to take an interest in fashion? That I'm not cool and hip like all your friends? Is that what you're saying?"

"No, of course not," I said lightly.

"Good." She smiled, and I could tell that for a moment she had been teasing me. Then she grew serious again.

"Modeling is a very superficial world, Cornelia. I'm not so sure I want my daughter to be part of it." She stopped to look at me carefully. "At least, not until you're a bit older, anyway."

She was going to say no. I *knew* I should have asked Dad first. Except I was sure he would have said, "Go ask your mother."

"Mom, do you think I'm a superficial person?" I asked.

My mom gave me a hug. "No, Cornelia, I don't think that."

"Well, do you think I'll suddenly become a superficial person, just because someone takes pictures of me for two days?"

There was a lengthy silence. I held my breath.

"You really want to do this?" she asked.

I nodded vigorously.

"And Hay Lin will be there?" she said.

"And probably one or two of the others. You can come, too, if you want." I felt my voice start to get higher as I got more and more excited. It was beginning to look as though this might actually happen!

"Well, I'm really busy next week," my mom said, "but maybe I can look in on you for an hour or so."

"You mean I can do it?" I shrieked.

"If your father agrees," she said.

He would, and we both knew it. Mom had been the real obstacle. I threw my arms around her and gave her a huge hug.

"Oh, *thank* you! Thank you, thank you, thank you!" I cried. "And I promise, I won't go all crazy and superficial. I'll . . . I'll read a philosophy book on the shoot, or something."

She laughed. "Maybe you should just try doing your homework instead."

☾ ☾ ◭ ◉ ☾

For the rest of that week, I was happy to think of nothing but Fairy-Tale Fantasies and the amazing dresses I'd be wearing. Acey Jones—still very put together and still very tan—had shown me sketches of the clothes, and they were breathtaking. But unfortunately, real life—in the botanical form—kept intruding. And at dinner one night the intrusion really hit home.

"The lot in front of our building is full of weeds," complained my father. "It looks terrible. Aren't we supposed to have someone who takes care of that?"

"I already called them," replied my mother, "and they said they came yesterday! Can you imagine? That's just impossible. It has to have been at least two weeks."

I looked down at my dinner plate and pretended to be interested in my food. The landscaping people really had been there the day before—I'd seen them. They had cut the grass and trimmed back the plants. It wasn't *their* fault the weeds were back already and the lawn was overgrown.

I was afraid that it might be my fault.

I had avoided Hanabaker Park all week and gone to school a different way, even though it took me longer. Now the trees along *that* particular street had bright green foliage, one month early. Mom's hibiscus had cracked another pot—thankfully I'd been the only one home when it happened. And the lawn in front of the main entrance to Sheffield Institute was suddenly covered by daffodils that no one remembered having planted.

On top of all the crazy plant behavior, for the past few nights I had been having the same awful dream night after night. It was vague—no images, really, just sensations, but it was still terrifying. The dream started with a weird feeling of vast emptiness. Like being in a desert. There was no life anywhere. And then the emptiness faded, and I heard a voice, a tiny, tiny voice inside my head that kept saying: *The worm . . . the worm is coming.* I had no idea what the voice was talking about. What worm? Even though I didn't know what was going on, the warning filled me with dread. The feeling filled me with a tidal wave of fear that was so strong I woke up, heart pounding, palms sweating.

It would take a while before I was calm enough to go back to sleep. I was tired from the sleepless nights; I was a wreck. This may have explained why, during Thursday's art class, I was more occupied with yawning and twirling my pencil than with sketching.

I heard Will clear her throat. "Er . . . Cornelia . . ." she whispered.

"What?" I said.

"Your pencil . . ." she began, pointing to my hand.

My pencil? What was wrong with my pencil?

Turns out, quite a lot was wrong with my pencil. Looking quickly around to make sure no one had noticed, I shoved the pencil in my bag and got out a pen instead. There was no way I could let Mrs. Wharton, our art teacher, and the rest of the class see that the yellow wooden pencil I'd been fiddling with had suddenly sprouted two tiny, perfect, pale green leaves.

Yes, something was certainly wrong in Heatherfield. The earth seemed to be bursting with extra energy—and that energy wasn't coming from my powers.

3

The next day I was in the middle of a serious fashion crisis. Would I wear the lavender sweater or the green one? I held up one, then the other, and looked critically at myself in the mirror each time. The green went well with the skirt I was wearing, but the lilac looked better with my complexion. It was a hard choice. I didn't want to arrive at Ladyhold looking like someone with no fashion sense.

"Cornelia! Hay Lin is here," my father called up to me. "And Mr. Jones said you had to be there by nine."

Green or lavender? Lavender or green?

"Just a second," I called back, tearing off the lavender sweater and putting on a new pink shirt. This was getting out of control. I had to calm down. I really couldn't tell if my latest choice was any better, but at that point, I just had to wear something.

"Cornelia!" My father was beginning to sound very impatient.

"I'm coming!" I yelled.

In the living room, Hay Lin was waiting for me. As usual, she looked amazing. She was dressed in striped tights and a miniskirt, with a pair of enormous goggles pushed back on top of her head. I envied her. Hay Lin didn't have to check fashion magazines like *Red Hot* to know what to wear—she had her own personal style that was always red-hot.

"Do I look okay?" I asked nervously.

"Pretty as a picture . . ." said my dad.

What did he know? He was my father. I turned and looked at Hay Lin.

"Seriously, is this okay?" I asked her.

"You look great," said Hay Lin, and smiled cheerfully.

I let out a small sigh of relief.

Lilian came bouncing into the room, chomping on a blueberry muffin. When she saw me, she stood still.

"You look so pretty," she said.

"Thanks, Lilian," I said. I was feeling better about my choice.

Suddenly, I felt clammy all over. What was *wrong* with me? How had I sunk so low as to consider the fashion opinions of my little sister? This was a horrible sign. I needed to get a grip.

"You look just like a real model!" Lilian added as she ran over to give me a hug.

"Oh, no!" Hay Lin gasped.

I followed Hay Lin's gaze and looked down at my shirt.

There were blue smears on my new pink shirt.

"Lilian!" I yelled. "*Look* what you did! This was the perfect outfit!"

"You look like Mrs. Gilberto's dog," she said. "You know, the one called Spot. Except Spot isn't pink and blue."

She seemed to have absolutely no clue what a disaster this was. I couldn't take it any longer. I lost my temper. "Do you have to be such a complete monkey, Lilian?" I yelled. "What's wrong with eating at the table?"

"I am *not* a monkey!" Lilian said, her eyes filling up with tears. Then she turned and ran out of the room.

"Cornelia!" my mom said sternly as she watched Lilian leave. "What did you say to your sister?"

"I didn't say anything," I replied. "Look what

she did to my shirt!" I pointed out the stain on my shirt.

For a moment, Mom looked as though she wanted to say something, but then she just sighed and said, "I suppose you had better go change. And hurry, your father has to be at work by nine-thirty."

"Lower your chin, please, and look straight into the camera."

"Turn your head, keep turning . . . good! Now hold it!"

"Raise your arm. A little higher."

"Keep it there, hold it, hold it . . ."

"Makeup! Can someone do *some*thing about that shine!"

"I said, raise that arm!"

"Don't smile, look *intense*."

"Darling, that's not intense, that's a frown!"

It was a few hours into the shoot, and it was not going the way I had expected. In fact, it was a living nightmare.

My arms ached. My cheeks ached. My head throbbed. My feet hurt. And they had put some stuff in my hair that was making my scalp itch uncontrollably.

"Cornelia! Please control yourself, and don't

scratch! Katie, will you fix her hair *again?*"

"Can we have a little more light here?"

I had imagined photo shoots as being a lot of fun. This one sure wasn't fun. It seemed as if everybody were ordering me around. People kept fussing with my makeup or my hair or the way the light fell on my face or the way I held my arm, or . . . a million other things that had to be just right for the picture of Mr. Sacharino's "wonderful creations."

And it was true—the creations *were* wonderful, which at least partly made up for all the other annoying stuff I had to do. At the moment, I was wearing a silky scarlet cloak and gown, which made me look as if I had been wrapped in huge rose petals. I was supposed to resemble Little Red Riding Hood, even though I don't think Little Red Riding Hood would have gotten very far into the dense woods in that outfit—the cloak would have gotten snagged on a tree or a shrub the second she wandered off the path.

"Darling," said the photographer, "do try and look a little more *impressed* with the wolf."

"I'm sorry," I said apologetically. "It's just . . . he doesn't look very dangerous."

It was true. Acey Jones was "acting" as the Wolf, and despite a bulky fur coat, he didn't look much like a hungry or scary predator. In fact, he looked more like a business executive afraid of catching a cold.

"Acey, could you sort of try and scare her more?"

Acey sighed and then gave me a hard glare that made me jump in surprise . . . and fear. It looked perfectly genuine and perfectly menacing.

"Good, and now move a little closer to her. . . ." the photographer started to say.

Acey took a step—and then tripped over a knot of vines that seemed to have sprung up out of nowhere, blocking his path.

Oh, no, I thought. Not this again! This can't be happening. I can't handle any more out-of-control spurts of plant growth.

Immediately, at least four people swooped in to help Acey up. He pushed their hands away and got up by himself, looking rumpled and absolutely furious. As the personal assistant to Mr. Sacharino, he was not used to being publicly embarrassed. The sunglasses he had been wearing had fallen off, and bits of vine clung to his gray fur coat.

"Why didn't somebody get rid of all these plants *before* we started shooting?" he snarled. "It's like a jungle out here!"

Some of the staff looked around, puzzled. I would have been, too. They were probably thinking that the place hadn't looked like such a jungle a moment before. And it hadn't. When Acey Jones snarled at me, some of the vines around us had instantly grown green tendrils that tried to grab at him.

Stop it, stop it, stop it, I whispered to myself. Why couldn't this just stop? What is happening?

The worm. The worm is coming. I heard that tiny voice again in my mind. I felt a wave of fear sweep over me.

The sound of the photographer's voice brought me back to the present. "Yes, all right, darling, now don't overdo it. We want excitement, not terror. Makeup, why is she so pale? Can you do something about that, please?"

"I'm sorry," I said breathlessly. "I think I have to sit down. . . ."

"Not there!" yelled the stylist in an anguished voice. But it was too late: my knees had buckled, and I collapsed in a heap on top of the vines and branches around me.

"Oh, my! Are you all right, darling?" cried the photographer.

"Sorry," I whispered, still feeling dizzy—not to mention slightly embarrassed. Just then I had a wave of fear just like in my dreams, only this time I wasn't dreaming.

"Let's break for lunch," said the photographer. "We'll get you something to eat, and hopefully you'll feel better. We can't have our star passing out on us, now, can we?" He nodded to Acey, who took that as his cue to get the food.

Giving me a withering look, Acey stalked off, muttering something about "amateurs, unknown nobodies, and silly, thoughtless girls." The brilliant smile he had flashed at me so often when he was persuading me to come to the shoot seemed to have vanished for good.

I was finally beginning to feel less faint, so I started to get up on my feet.

"Wait, be careful. . . ." warned the stylist, who was concerned more about the dress, of course, than about me.

"Is the dress all right?" I asked the stylist. I would have felt even worse if I had destroyed it when I fell.

She looked me over. "Well, yes . . . everything seems perfectly fine," she said in a perplexed tone as she examined the dress.

But I had a sneaking suspicion that everything wasn't fine. Not in the least.

€ € ◭ ◉ €

"This is so cool!" Taranee said as she looked around the photo shoot. I could tell that Taranee was impressed with all of the photography equipment.

"Are you having fun?" Irma asked me excitedly, as she examined the large suitcase full of makeup on a chair nearby. My friends had swung by the shoot to lend me their support, and, of course, to check out the scene. It wasn't every day that they got to see a real live photo shoot.

"Well," I said. "I don't know about fun." We were still on lunch break, but I wasn't feeling very hungry.

Hungry. Hungry. The worm is hungry.

"Cornelia! What's wrong? You're shaking!" Will said, grabbing my hand.

"I don't know what's wrong with me!" I whispered. It was true—my hands were shaking.

"Are you nervous about the shoot?" Hay Lin asked gently.

"No. Yes. But that's not it." I hesitated, then decided I had to tell them. "I've been having these dreams . . . nightmares, really." I tried to describe what the dreams were like, but it was hard to explain. "Now I seem to be having them in the daytime, too. Do you guys think I'm going crazy?"

Irma gave me a knowing look. "Could be," she said. "Yes. In fact, I'm sure that's what's going on."

"Irma!" Will said, jabbing her side with one elbow.

"Ouch! Oh, come on," Irma said. "I was only teasing. . . ."

"Well, maybe she's not in the mood to be teased!" Will said sternly.

But to be honest, I kinda was. Even though I usually hated her teasing, there was something reassuring about Irma's joking just then. If Irma had thought for even a moment that I really might be close to losing it, she would never have joked.

"Cornelia, seriously," Taranee said, "you are just about the sanest and most sensible person I know."

"Fine, then, but if I'm not crazy, what's going on?" I asked.

"Weird stuff," said Hay Lin, as if that simple response explained anything. She had witnessed the episode of the vines growing randomly earlier, so she knew that something strange was definitely happening.

"Do you think we should talk to the Oracle?" asked Will. "He always seems to have an answer—or at least a suggestion."

"I honestly don't know," I said. "What are we going to say to him? I mean, we can't go to the Oracle every time one of us has a nightmare. We should be stronger than that."

"I think this counts as a bit more than a nightmare," said Hay Lin matter-of-factly.

"Yeah, but still . . ." my voice trailed off.

We sat in silence for a little while, all separately trying to think of a plan that would make everything better. I was having no luck.

"Er . . . Cornelia?" Hay Lin cleared her throat. "Could you let go of the plate? My peanuts are sprouting. . . ."

Horrified, I snatched my hand away. "This has got to stop!" I said loudly.

Suddenly, a heap of glossy photos landed on the table in front of the five of us. We all jumped back, startled.

"Ms. Hale," said Acey Jones in an acid tone. "Look at *these*."

I looked at the photos. They were shots from that morning's session, some of me in Ladyhold's ballroom in a long, blue, princess-type gown, and some of me in the Little Red Riding Hood outfit I was still wearing.

"They look great!" said Taranee enthusiastically.

Acey Jones scowled at her. He reached across and picked a clear, sharp, brilliant close-up out of the pile.

"Great?" he asked. "They are completely useless! Look at this!"

In the photo he held up to me, strange green sparks appeared to be floating around my face. Acey Jones pulled another photograph from the pile and shoved it in my face.

"And this!" he yelled.

More green specks on the photograph.

"And this. And this! Every single one!" he bellowed.

He was right. They were there—in every photograph that had been taken of me—tiny green flashes of light, in my hair, around my face, and dancing along the edges of the gowns I was wearing.

"We checked the film. We checked the lenses. We checked the lights and the cameras. We checked everything," he said. "I'm not sure what tricks you are playing here, but these games will not be tolerated."

"I'm sorry," I said. "But I really don't see . . ."

"A whole day of shooting, wasted, Ms. Hale, because of you," Acey said. "Do you realize how much that costs?"

"But it's not . . ." I started to respond. Acey didn't even bother to hear me out.

"I don't know exactly what is going on with you," Acey said. "I'm not sure I want to know. But I do know that we were wrong to hire an amateur. You're fired, Ms. Hale."

4

I ran through the park surrounding Ladyhold until I reached the gates. I staggered to a stop, my sides heaving and my eyes blinded by my own tears.

I wasn't crying just about being fired. I was crying about everything—all the strange things that had been happening and the feelings I couldn't explain. You would think someone who had power over earth, someone who was a Guardian, would have had more self-control. But I didn't.

Sometimes it seemed that my power brought me nothing but pain. In a way, I blamed my power for taking Elyon, my best friend, away from me. Now she ruled over Meridian and would definitely never again be sitting next to me in class sharing secrets, or sketching in her notebook while we stayed up late at night talking.

And then there was Caleb. The love of my life, who happened to live in another world and was the leader of a rebel resistance. Why couldn't I be like Will and fall in love with someone like Matt Olsen? Someone I could be *with* every day, in my own world. But no, I had to go and fall for a boy who would never just stop by for a slice of pizza or take me to a school dance.

Sad. So sad. Sorry.

There it was again. That tiny, tiny voice that was more a feeling than a sound. A feeling of sorrow and regret.

I blinked away the last of my angry tears.

Floating in front of my face, no more than ten inches from my nose, was a green spark. A small, glowing, green light which somehow had a voice. Once again, I felt confused. Nothing was making sense any more.

"Who are you?" I blurted out.

There was no real answer. Just a general feeling of affection that seemed to translate into the word *friend*.

Then I noticed something. There were more than just one of the glowing green specks in front of me. In fact, there were many more. Hundreds of tiny sparks now hovered all around me. But the one flitting in front of my nose was the biggest of the bunch—more of a patch than a spark.

Around me, the meadow, which had just before appeared barren, exploded in a mass of glowing buttercups. I was blinded by the brilliant gold display. And the bare trees were no longer bare. New spring leaves curled softly at the tip of every twig, making the trees burst with green.

"It's *you*," I said, the realization suddenly dawning on me. "You've been doing this. All the growing."

"Cornelia? Cornelia, are you all right?"

I jumped at the sound of my name. It was Will. I had been so wrapped up in talking to the sparks that I hadn't heard her or the others approach.

"I'm okay," I called back. "How did you find me here?"

My four friends came into the meadow and gathered around me.

"All we had to do was follow the path of green," said Hay Lin. "Cornelia, maybe your power really has gone wild on you. . . ." She made a gesture toward the buttercups and blooming trees.

"No, it hasn't," I said, relieved to be able to say so and mean it. I was in total control. "Patch and his friends are doing it. Look . . ."

At that moment, every single spark of green vanished.

"Oh, you shy little things," I murmured gently, trying not to scare the green sparks away. "Come on out and meet my friends!"

There was no response. Taranee had a look on her face that clearly said she thought I might *really* be going crazy.

"I think they're afraid," I said. "Will, would you show them the Heart? I think that might help them trust you."

"Show who?" Will asked, looking around with a confused expression on her face.

"The little green sparks, I suppose you could call them," I said. "Somehow, they are connected to all this crazy growing going on around me. They caused the buttercups to bloom and the trees to sprout."

"I guess it wouldn't hurt to try," Will said.

Will brought out the Heart of Candracar. And as it always did, the Heart gave me strength.

Now, the orb rested in her hand, glowing gently. The Heart embodied all the natural elements in perfect balance. Patch and his friends were clearly a force of nature, and I thought they might be comforted by the Heart's presence, just as I was.

As soon as the Heart appeared, there was a kind of squeak of surprise.

Patch was back—along with about a thousand of his friends. They were all dancing around the Heart—whirling, leaping joyfully, in swirls of glowing green. I laughed. I couldn't help it. Not because it was funny, but because they were so full of joy.

"Wow!" said Hay Lin. "Check that out!"

For a moment, Irma was speechless. She just stared at the green sparks with her mouth open.

Finally, Irma got her voice back. "Well, if you are crazy, so am I," she said. "I'm seeing little green men!"

"They're definitely not men," objected Taranee. "They're . . . they're just lights."

"But they are people. Or beings, anyway," Hay Lin added.

"People," I said firmly. "They have feelings and thoughts just like people." I held out my palm. "Patch? Patch, could you hold still for a moment? We'd like to look at you."

And just like that, Patch rested in my cupped palm.

"That's Patch?" Will asked, peering into my hand.

"I just call him that because he's a bigger

patch of green than the others." But, judging by the feeling of acceptance I was getting, it seemed "Patch" was an okay name by him.

"Where are you from, Patch?" asked Hay Lin gently.

Suddenly, he paled. A feeling of fear hit me.

The worm. The worm is coming.

The fear was overwhelming. I felt my legs get weak, and I sat down abruptly. The damp ground soaked into the thin fabric of my dress, but I was too weak and upset to care.

"Hey, they're gone," said Irma. "Where did all the green guys go?"

Irma was right. The green sparks had vanished—except for Patch, who clung stubbornly to my hand.

Help. Please help.

"I think that something awful must be happening wherever they come from," I said. "My nightmares must be a sort of message."

I suddenly understood what was happening. Patch was asking for my help.

I looked at each of my friends' faces. They, too, looked concerned.

"I think it's time we went to see the Oracle," I said.

The five of us put our hands on the Heart.

"Heart of Candracar," said Will quietly. "Bring us before the Oracle."

Our amazing transformation into Guardians began. I felt the familiar surge of energy, and the welcome magical change.

Almost immediately, the green meadow, yellow buttercups, and new trees all vanished in a blur. Now, in their place, there were a vaulted ceiling and pillars taller than any of the trees that had surrounded us.

"Welcome, Guardians."

This was the standard greeting from the Oracle. By this point, we had all learned to expect it whenever we arrived in Candracar. The welcome felt like more than mere words. It felt like an affirmation of acceptance and belonging.

"Patch and his friends are in great trouble," I began, unable to contain myself any longer.

"You call him Patch?" the Oracle asked, with a note of humor in his voice.

"I know it's not his real name. . . ." I started to explain.

"Do not worry. He accepts it. 'Patch' will do."

"We want to help him, but I don't even know where he comes from," I said.

"He comes from a world named Phylia. It was once lush and green with growing things, but since Patch and his people fled, it is in danger of becoming a wasteland. You see, Patch and his fellow beings are the very essence of growth. Without them, few things can bloom."

"I guess that's why things in Heatherfield have been blooming like crazy," Taranee pointed out matter-of-factly.

"He was probably drawn to Cornelia because of her connection to the powers of the earth. He knew she could aid him in his quest."

I knew there was more that the Oracle had to tell me. "There is something he fears, some enemy that threatens him and the other green sparks, isn't there?" I asked. I needed to know everything if I were going to be of any help to Patch.

"Yes."

I waited, but the Oracle apparently had no more to say about the enemy. As always, his messages were straight to the point.

"Can we go to Phylia and help Patch face this enemy?" I asked.

"If that is what you wish."

"Well, we do. Don't we?" I looked around at my friends, who were all nodding their heads in agreement.

I must warn you—I doubt many of the sparks

will have the courage to follow you. They do not have Patch's strength. Knowing this, do you still wish to go to Phylia, and face that which caused Patch and his kin to flee in terror?"

"Yes," I heard myself say boldly.

"Very well, then. Good luck, Guardians."

And then, in a flash, we were no longer in Candracar.

Our journey to Phylia had begun. We knew we had a mission. But what awaited us was unknown . . . and that was terrifying.

5

The ground was gray, and a harsh wind rustled through piles of dead leaves.

"Talk about bleak," whispered Will.

It was not completely desolate. There were trees, but they were leafless. And in the fields on either side, dried-out wheat and barley stalks stood.

"Anyone else thinking maybe we should have brought lunch with us?" asked Irma.

Typical Irma, I thought. Always trying to lighten up dark situations. This time, though, it didn't work—no one even smiled.

A loud wailing sound came from across the barren meadow. The five of us looked around with worried expressions. It sounded like a wounded child.

"Let's find that child," said Will, ignoring

Irma's remark. Will was much better at letting Irma's quips bounce off her. Right now, she was in total leader mode. "I don't know about you, but I can't stand to listen to that crying for much longer," Will added.

We walked through the meadow and came upon a desolate town. It was downright depressing. At one point, the town must have been pretty and prosperous. The traces of its former state were still there—stores and pretty houses lined the street. But where they once might have been warm and welcoming, they now had an abandoned look to them.

Despite the sad condition of the town, there were still people working in barren fields and dusty streets. The people looked as gray and lifeless as the soil.

Even though people wandered through the town, it was eerily quiet. In the town square, by a fountain that leaked a mere trickle of water, some women did their laundry. But the women didn't talk as they worked, or sing or laugh. And the weirdest part of all was that despite the fact that we were complete strangers, they just glanced at us before they went back to their washing.

From another part of the square, a trader, who appeared to be selling wooden bowls and boxes, occasionally raised his voice to call out: "Pretty bowls and boxes, best quality, two for a penny. Great deal on such pretty bowls and boxes."

His voice was dull and hopeless. He knew he wouldn't sell anything. He was just going through the motions out of habit.

Through the strange, eerie hush, we could still hear the wailing of the child.

I walked across the square to the man selling the boxes and bowls. As I approached, he raised his head; suddenly his face filled with hopeful interest.

"A pretty girl," he said with a tired smile. "Such a pretty girl needs a pretty box to keep her pretty things in!"

I shook my head and softly said no. I felt bad not helping him, but whatever was going wrong in this town, buying one of his boxes certainly wouldn't cure it.

"Whose child is crying like that?" I asked.

The man's eyes grew dull again, and he dropped his head hopelessly into his hands.

"Mara, the potter's," he said, his voice drained of any enthusiasm he might have previously had. "The child's been crying like that since noon. But there's no help for it."

"Where does Mara live?" I asked, hoping my

voice didn't give away my anxiety.

"Down over there," he said, nodding. "The house with the blue door and the white brick chimney."

"Thank you," I replied. Turning, I looked at my friends and smiled encouragingly. They knew what we had to do. Without another word, we started walking toward the house with the white chimney and the crying child inside.

🥚🥚🥚🥚🥚

When we arrived at the small house, we knocked on the front door. "Come in," a woman's tired voice said.

Irma slowly pushed the door open. A dark-haired woman, sitting by a potter's wheel, looked up as we entered.

"Who are you?" she asked, apparently too tired to be more polite.

"Strangers," I said, avoiding a more complex explanation. "We heard the child crying and thought we might be able to help."

The child who had been the source of all the noise crouched on a cot next to the wheel. He was a small, dark-haired boy whose skin was pale from weeping.

"Help?" his mother said. "That would be great! Just get out the porridge, the bread, and the honey, and I'll offer you some of my best cider." She laughed, but it wasn't a happy sound. It was an angry, bitter sound. Sighing, she looked at the boy. "He's crying because he's hungry, the poor thing, and there's nothing to be done about it. Not until tonight at the Sharing, and what he'll get then won't be enough to satisfy an ant."

Her hands never stopped working the clay as she talked. With precision, she molded the clay in a few motions. I watched, fascinated, as a beautiful pot grew between her slender and graceful hands.

"You mean you have no food in this house?" I asked, when I finally pulled my eyes away from her hands.

She shot me a dark, furious look. "If I had food, do you think I would let my child cry with hunger?"

"No . . . I . . . I didn't mean it like that. It's just that . . ." I thought of the kitchen in my house, with its overflowing cupboards and a refrigerator always stocked full of goodies. Hungry, for me, usually meant the interval between thinking about being hungry and making myself a sandwich. "Where I come from, there is usually plenty of food," I finally said, trying to justify myself.

"Then you must come from very far away,"

said Mara, looking only a little less furious. "And trust me, you'll regret you ever came to this miserable place." She raised one hand to push back a lock of dark hair, leaving a smear of reddish clay on her forehead. "This town used to be called Plenty, you know. But not anymore." She smiled her bitter, dark smile again. "Now, we call it Hunger."

We all dug into our pockets, but the most we came up with was two foil-wrapped pieces of chewing gum.

"That's not going to help," sighed Will. "He'd choke on it."

Mara's child had finally stopped wailing and was looking at the bright silver gum-wrappers we held in our hands. His eyes were huge in his pale face.

"This is ridiculous. What good are we if we can't somehow create a little food?" I said angrily. I turned to Mara. "Do you have any vegetables?" I asked her. "Peas, beans, anything? It doesn't matter."

"Nothing that's still fresh," she said. "The old vegetable patch is out back." She nodded in the direction of the back door and at the barren yard beyond.

"Perfect," I said. "This should take no time."

I walked out the back door and into the small walled garden. Or, more accurately, into what might have once been a garden. There was a tree that looked as though it might have been an apple or pear tree once upon a time. Besides that, there was a peach tree and a small gray patch of soil with a few withered bean stalks and pea plants sticking out of it.

I walked straight up to the peach tree and put my palms against its slender trunk. Now, I had thought, let's see what a little earth magic can do. I closed my eyes and called on my element, willing it to nourish the tree and somehow make it grow new fruit.

It was actually much harder to do than I had thought it would be. As a matter of fact, at first it seemed downright impossible. Usually my power responded quickly and willingly. This time, there was nothing but a horrible, sluggish feeling inside my lungs that made me cough so badly I had to let go of the tree. I felt like I was suffocating.

Hay Lin, who had followed me into the garden, rested a hand on my shoulder.

"What's wrong?" she asked.

"Everything," I gasped, trying to catch my breath. I looked around the yard looking for some sign of life. "The earth . . . it's like it's not even there. It's like there's nothing good and living left!"

"How can there be no earth?" Hay Lin asked, her face filled with fear. "It's one of the four elements! It can't just disappear!"

"Well . . . maybe it's not completely gone," I said. "But it's definitely not here."

I had finally caught my breath, so I put my hands on the tree again. This time I was a little more prepared for the wave of sickness that hit me when I began. I gritted my teeth, closed my eyes, and kept calling on my power.

Finally, I thought I felt something. There was a tiny tugging deep in the tree. It was a small response, considering that the effort was making sweat run down my face, but at least it was something. I opened my eyes. A tiny bud appeared on the withered-looking branch. It had a long way to go before it resembled an edible peach.

"I could use a little help from Patch and his friends right about now," I said, feeling my knees wobble with exhaustion.

"The Oracle said they probably wouldn't dare come back here," Will said matter-of-factly.

"I know." I sighed sadly. "It was a nice thought, though."

Just as I was about to close my eyes again, a

single small green spark landed on my hand. For the first time since we had arrived, there was a little bit of green in the barren garden.

"Patch!" I said, smiling. Suddenly, I felt stronger and more hopeful. "You came!"

I felt a wave of warmth and affection wash over me, followed by a small shiver of apprehension. I knew Patch was happy to see me, but that didn't make him any less scared. He had taken a huge risk in following us there. None of the other sparks had made the journey.

"Don't worry," I said to him soothingly. "I'll watch out for you. I promise I won't let anything happen to you."

The trembling eased a little, and Patch's glow grew greener.

"Now, Patch, I have a very hungry child who'd love some food. Think you could help me with that?"

Help tree. Help child.

"That's what I hope happens," I said, looking at Patch and nodding in encouragement.

Patch bobbed in the air above the tree for a moment and then suddenly seemed to melt right into the bark.

Now. Help tree now.

Here we go again, I thought. I closed my eyes

and, using all my strength, summoned the powers of the earth one more time.

"It's working!" I heard Hay Lin cry. "Keep going, keep going. . . ."

I cringed. Easy for her to say. Hay Lin didn't have to pull at the dull, reluctant power that wanted nothing to do with this place. I closed my eyes and concentrated, willing all my strength into that tree. I couldn't give up now.

"Cornelia, you did it!" I heard Will cry triumphantly.

I sagged against the tree, coughing. Slowly, I opened my eyes . . . and gasped. I had done it! The bud had become a peach—a very small peach, but at least it was ripe.

"Pick it," I said hoarsely to Irma. "And give it to Mara."

"Are you all right?" Hay Lin asked, an anxious look on her face.

Of course, I wanted to say yes, but I was far from being all right.

"Er . . . not quite," I said. And then my legs buckled, and I collapsed at the root of the tree.

"Will!" called Hay Lin sharply. "Will, we need help!"

Will had the Heart of Candracar in her palm, and she let it rest against my chest.

"Lie still," she told me. "Let the Heart do the work for a little while. You've worn yourself out."

It seemed ridiculous, but I *had* worn myself out, in five minutes, over one little peach. It didn't seem possible that I could be so tired.

"Guess I'm not much of a Guardian," I muttered weakly.

"Don't be ridiculous," said Taranee. "You're a great Guardian, and great at controlling earth. There's just something really wrong with the earth around here. Anybody can see that. It's like the soil is exhausted."

"I know what that feels like," I whispered. I felt as if I'd never be able to move again. And, to be honest, I didn't really want to move—for a long time.

I was about to say more when a sudden fear hit me. "Patch! Is he all right? Where is he? Does anyone see him?"

"Don't worry," said Will, pushing me back down. "He's right here, and he's fine. See?"

Patch was practically on top of the Heart. And while he did look okay, he was glowing a lot less brightly than he had been a few moments before.

"Poor Patch," I murmured. "You had to work a lot just now, didn't you?"

Tree better. Will help child.

The Heart had made me stronger, so I stood up and walked the short distance to Mara's house.

"We found you a peach," I said brightly upon entering from the garden.

A startled look crossed Mara's face and she looked at us, then at the peach, as if she couldn't believe what she was seeing. Speechless, she took the peach and brought it close to her face, sniffing it as if she couldn't believe the fruit was real. From the cot, the child's eyes followed the peach hungrily. He stretched out a thin hand, but did not beg.

Mara looked at me with a combination of disbelief and hope. "Is there any way you could get . . . another one?" she asked in a whisper. The look on her face broke my heart.

"Not right now," I said. "At least, not until tomorrow."

"I understand. Thank you for this, though." Standing up, she walked over and washed her clay-smeared hands at the water pump, then found a knife in a drawer. Carefully, she cut the peach in half.

"Here, Taddy," she said, handing half of the peach to her son. "You can have this, and the rest we'll bring to the Sharing tonight."

"I . . . I meant for you two to have all of it," I said. Half a peach was not enough to feed a hungry child.

Mara nodded. "I know. That's nice of you. But what we have, we share. If we didn't, half of us would have starved by now."

It was impossible not to admire her strength. She had to be hungry, too, but the only indulgence she allowed herself was to lick the fingers that had held the peach.

"What's happened to your town?" I asked. "Why is it so barren?" I had to ask, even though I imagined such a question would seem strange to the woman.

She stared at me as if she couldn't believe I didn't know. "Caroc, of course," she replied. "Caroc the Worm."

6

Standing on a barren hillside with Mara and Taddy, we looked down at Caroc. Or at least, we tried to.

He was so huge it took me a while to really see him. I know that sounds strange, but it's true. My eyes were expecting something merely monster-sized, not something the size of a small mountain range.

"Is that . . . that huge thing . . . him?" I asked Mara.

She nodded and shifted Taddy on her hip so she had one arm free for pointing. "There," she said. "And there. And there's a coil. I think his head is somewhere to the south right now."

I couldn't believe my eyes.

"This is not good," said Taranee in a small voice. "I don't even like *little* bugs."

Caroc's body had to be more than a mile long. He lay coiled around a castle, where, according to Mara, he held the ruler of the realm, Prince Florian, captive. Lying there, Caroc's sickly gray skin blended into the soil, which was one reason it had taken us so long to spot him.

"How do you know he is causing the destruction?" I asked Mara, when I had finally recovered from the shock of seeing Caroc for the first time. The mere sight of him had made me speechless.

"Simple. He eats everything. He eats the land itself. Every day, he swallows up another garden, another half of a field, another grove of trees. Once he gets hold of something, its gone. He never releases his grip, and he *never* stops swallowing. He's an absolute monster. He breathes out poisonous air, and its almost like he oozes venom. Oh, yes, he is definitely the cause. This land was rich and healthy until he came."

"Why your town?" Irma asked. "And why does he never move far from the castle?"

"I don't think even Caroc knows why he is here anymore. There is only mindless greed," Mara said. Then she added, "But once, he was the prince's cousin."

I gasped. There was no way that Mara could be telling us the truth. "Are you telling me that

that . . . monster down there is a relative of your prince? That it was—human?"

"Yes. That thing was once Duke Caroc. A hungry, greedy man, who hoped to gain the throne through his sorcery. Before that, though, he tried to raise an army, but the people of Phylia wanted nothing to do with it, and his power was not great enough to force them into obedience. Then he decided that since he could not raise an army, he had to become one himself.

"Using his magical powers, he took the shape of a giant worm so that he could surround and besiege the castle all by himself. Then he demanded Prince Florian's surrender. But our Prince is a strong and determined man, and he refused to give up."

"You mean, this could end if Prince Florian surrendered?" I asked, in disbelief.

Mara shook her head sadly. "It's too late. I heard he tried to give up a few months ago. He couldn't stand seeing his people in pain any longer. The prince wanted to ease their suffering. But by then Caroc was too far gone and couldn't understand words like 'throne' and 'prince' and 'sovereignty.' All that creature is capable of understanding now is greed . . . and hunger."

Mara stopped speaking and we all stared

down at Caroc in silence. It was hard to imagine that something so ugly and evil could ever have been human. A sudden wind blew the stench of the snake into our faces, and I coughed at the rancid sharpness of the scent. Taddy cried out and began rubbing at his eyes and nose.

"I can't stay here," Mara said with a note of fear in her voice. "I brought you here because you asked me to, but this is an evil place, and I can't bear it here any longer."

Taking one last look at Caroc, she shuddered, turned, and began walking down the hill, toward the town they now called Hunger.

I kept my eyes locked on Caroc. There was nothing alive in the space between him and us. No trees, no plants, no animals or birds or even insects. My nose, eyes, and throat burned from the fumes he emitted.

"You'd need a gas mask and a rubber suit to try and even get near him," muttered Will.

She was right. Even this far away from him, I felt overwhelmed and slightly ill. There was no way I could use my power if I had to deal with Caroc's stench.

"Too bad I left mine at home," Irma joked.

"I guess it's a good thing you have me," Hay Lin said, trying to sound as upbeat as Irma. "I can give us plenty of clean air—better than any gas mask."

"But he's just so big," Taranee said, shuddering. "How can we fight something that big when we're this small? It's impossible!"

"He's got to have a weak spot of some kind," said Will.

"*Sure* he does," countered Irma, sarcastically. "Have you seen him? Does he *look* like he has a weak spot?"

"Oh, come on," I said, feeling courage well up inside of me. "We control earth, air, fire, water, and energy. I'd say we pack quite a punch, don't you think?"

We had to do something. For Taddy and Mara's sake. For Phylia.

Will looked at me and smiled. "You're right," she said. "Let's give him a dose of real W.I.T.C.H. power!"

That was the moment I'd been waiting for since we'd arrived. Before our eyes, Will transformed. Her jeans and sweatshirt disappeared and were replaced with a purple and blue body-hugging outfit—complete with fluttery wings. She was taller, sleeker, stronger, and infinitely more *powerful*. Done with her transformation, Will stretched her arms above her head for a moment, getting ready for action. You could feel her power just by looking at her.

I smiled. Now it was our turn. A moment later, we had all transformed. We were no longer five ordinary-looking girls, tired and dirty and a bit confused; now we were truly Guardians—and it felt great.

"Mmmm . . ." murmured Irma, enjoying the change. "That's better. I don't know about you girls, but *I'm* definitely ready to go kick some worm!"

Getting within kicking distance of Caroc, however, was far from easy. Hay Lin was there to make sure we had clean air to breathe, rather than the fumes of Caroc, which surrounded us like a heavy mist. But as we got closer to the worm, I could see that the task of providing air was becoming harder for her.

"Are you okay?" I asked, glancing over at Hay Lin.

She nodded grimly. "I'm fine," she said. "But the closer we get to that thing . . . well, air just doesn't want to come around here."

The ground was slippery now with some sort of gray slime, and I realized my feet had gotten really hot. Standing awkwardly on one leg, I checked the sole of my boot. It was smoking slightly, and had begun to bubble.

"This stuff is like acid," I exclaimed, showing the others my burned boot. "It's eating through the soles of my shoes!"

"Mine, too," said Taranee, checking. "We have to do something before it gets to our actual feet!"

Always the drama queen, Irma raised her hands in a powerful stance. "I'll clear a path for us," she said, conjuring up a waterspout. "Stand back."

She directed the water to slice away the slime, leaving a clear, wet, but slime-free trail for us to follow. Even though Irma and I don't always get along, I had to hand it to her—she definitely had a flair when it came to using her power. And she wasn't afraid to show it off.

"Thanks, water girl," said Will gratefully.

"Any time," replied Irma with a cheerful grin. "I can make a waterslide, too. Maybe put a pool over there, import a few palm trees . . . we'll have the tourist trade back up and running in no time. It'll be a real resort destination."

I gazed at the bare, dead landscape and tried to imagine the pools and palm trees. It was hard to picture, but Irma's sense of humor was relentless, and I had to smile. At least the worm wasn't sucking the life out of Irma!

With Irma's path to protect our feet, we kept walking until we arrived at the worm. He was about three times bigger than me, and covered in hard scales. "Still want to kick him?" I asked Irma.

"Doesn't look as if it would do much good." She grimaced. "But, hey, whatever we do, I want him to see us doing it. Let's find the face of this beast!"

We picked a direction and started walking along the length of Caroc's body. Up close, he looked way too large to be a living thing.

I had been so distracted examining Caroc, I hadn't noticed that the slime had begun to burn my shoes again. When I felt a tingling sensation on the bottoms of my feet, I squealed. "Irma, that stuff is getting on my boots again!"

"Hold on a sec," she cried. She closed her eyes and concentrated. Eventually, a small jet of water appeared, but it was slow and sluggish, nothing like her normal, energetic geysers. She looked around with an embarrassed expression.

"Sorry," she muttered. "I guess water doesn't want to come here, either."

"It's good enough. Thanks, Irma," said Will soothingly.

We continued walking. And walking. And walking.

"How big *is* this creature?" asked Irma with a disgusted sigh.

"Mara said his head was somewhere toward the south," I said, remembering the earlier conversation. "Could we be walking in the wrong direction?"

Taranee squinted at the sun, barely visible through the mist of vapors surrounding Caroc. "No," she said. "We're heading south." She looked around. "It can't be that far now, we've—"

Suddenly, she stopped talking, her body frozen in shock.

Turning, I, too, stood still, unable to move.

In front of us, a deep, dark hole had appeared. It was a strange and cavelike hole, with rows of spikes above and below, and a ridged ceiling just like . . . just like the roof of some monstrous mouth.

"Oh, no," I whispered, realizing exactly what we were looking at.

"*Run!*" screamed Will.

None of us was about to argue. The mouth was moving quickly toward us, and the spikes on top were coming down, ready to devour us.

We raced across the slippery ground, running

for our lives. Hay Lin took off from the ground altogether and simply flew. I wished I could have done the same, but my wings, unfortunately, were only for decoration. They were absolutely no help in emergency situations. There was a crunching sound behind us as Caroc's jaws closed around a chunk of earth, and a rumble as he prepared to swallow. My stomach clenched at the unappealing sound. It was pure luck, though, that he swallowed just dirt and rocks, and not us.

At that moment, I just wanted to keep running all the way back to Hunger, or Heatherfield, for that matter. My legs were tired, and my lungs felt as if they were about to burst. So I stopped. And turned.

Perhaps a hundred feet away, a huge, triangular head was turned our way. A pair of pale, mud-colored eyes, bigger than windows, stared at us hungrily. Far behind the head, the tip of Caroc's tail could be seen, twitching slowly from side to side, like a cat on the prowl.

"Well, we found his head," gasped Irma. "So, who wants to go after him first?"

Not surprisingly, nobody volunteered.

"I think it would be smarter to hit him together," Will finally said. "With *everything* we've got."

I nodded. "It's the only way to cause any damage." After all, we were at our strongest when we combined our powers. Considering Caroc's size, I figured, the more power, the better.

Irma called on water. Hay Lin called on air. Fire danced around Taranee, and pure energy radiated from Will. And I put my hand flat against the ground, asking the poor abused earth of Phylia to fight back.

"Now," said Will, when we were all ready. "*Now.*"

We focused on Caroc and hit him with every bit of power, every ounce of strength that we had. Wind, flame, and water pounded him, rocks and lightning scoured his hide.

At first, he pulled back, looking almost surprised. Then his eyes lit up with a strange, greedy light. And then he opened his mouth and swallowed all our power.

Stunned, we stared at the monstrous worm.

"He ate it," said Will faintly.

Even as we looked, we could see him swelling, puffing up to an even greater size, fed by the power full of magic we had poured into him.

"I hope it gives him a terrible stomachache," said Irma savagely. "I hope he bursts or something."

Once again, I found myself agreeing with Irma. Unfortunately, Caroc looked fine—for a giant worm.

"How are we going to beat him?" asked Taranee, a tremor in her voice. "How can we possibly beat something like that if it eats our powers for fun?"

"I don't know," said Will. "Maybe we can't. Maybe this is the one mission we don't win."

My hand hurt. I looked down at my palm and grimaced. Where my hand had touched the soiled ground, the skin was seared and red, with big, painful blisters.

"This place is so sick," I whispered. "I'm not even sure it can ever be healed."

Suddenly, a small green glow was dancing in the air above my injured hand, bathing it in light that somehow lessened the pain.

"Patch!" I said, surprised and grateful. "Patch, you shouldn't be here. This place is too dangerous for you. . . ." Even though I was telling him to go away, I was really happy to see him. His fear was so strong it was almost tangible, but his trust and friendship were even stronger.

Help. Help the earth.

It was both a promise and a plea.

"I will," I murmured. "I will."

But I didn't see how. The worm was huge, voracious, and if we hit him again, he would simply swallow more power. There seemed no end to his greed.

No end . . .

I suddenly remembered what Mara had said: *Once he has hold of something, it is lost. He never releases his grip, he never stops swallowing—I don't think he can.*

"Girls," I said slowly, a smile spreading over my face. "I think I have a plan. . . ."

7

"Paint?" said Mara. "What do you want with a bucket of paint?"

I realized my request probably sounded extremely odd to Mara. We had just come back from facing Caroc and here we were asking for paint. She probably thought we were crazy. "Two paint colors would be great, or, better yet, three."

"Well, I have my pottery paints. But they are difficult to mix. I wouldn't want to waste them," Mara replied.

I looked her straight in the eye. "Is getting rid of Caroc important enough?"

She started to laugh, then stopped herself when she saw that I wasn't kidding.

"You're serious?" Mara asked.

"Very serious," I replied.

"Well, then, take whatever you want. Only . . ."

She hesitated, as if wondering how to say what she thought.

"Yes?" I prompted.

"I saw you make that peach. I know that you girls are more than what you seem. But Caroc is a terrible enemy. Please be careful!"

I nodded solemnly. "We will."

We spent the next half hour preparing the paints. Finally, after everything was organized, we headed out to face Caroc—and, hopefully, save Phylia.

We were halfway down the street when Mara suddenly came running after us.

"Wait," she cried, knotting a shawl around her shoulders. "I'm coming with you."

"But, Mara, it—" I began, before she interrupted me.

"Whatever it is you're going to do, someone needs to see it. Someone needs to know what really happened."

"What about Taddy?" I couldn't imagine Mara leaving her young son alone. He was too young to be left alone.

"I left him with my neighbor," she said.

"No, what I meant was—" But I couldn't bring myself to say, *what if you never come back.* "He needs his mother, Mara."

"And he'll have her," she said simply. "When I get back. I'm not planning on taking any chances. But someone from Hunger should be there when you face Caroc."

We were now passing through the square, and I noticed that the dull-eyed peddlers were starting to look a little less dull.

"What's going on, Mara?" cried the one who had tried to sell me a box earlier. "Are you off to see the worm?"

"Might be," replied Mara tersely.

"Good luck to you, then. You'll need it."

A couple of women added their good wishes. But one woman just looked at us with a dark glare.

"Why are you doing this? You're just going to make things worse," the woman growled.

"What do you mean, Ina?" asked Mara sharply.

"People should just leave that beast alone," the woman spat. "Then maybe he would leave us alone, too."

"But Ina, he's destroying us!" Mara said. "Closing your eyes and pretending he isn't there isn't going to make him go away. We have to do something!"

"Aye, well, just don't go making him mad is all

I say. What if he decides to leave the castle and comes looking for the people in town?"

One of the other women straightened up and put her hands on her hips. "Oh, Ina—stop being such a coward," the woman said. "If Mara and her new friends are going to try and do something about the worm, I'm going with them." Having made her announcement, she began to take off her apron.

"But . . ." I stared at the woman. I was happy people wanted to help, but, like everyone else in Hunger, she was very skinny and looked incredibly weak. What did she think she would be able to do if Caroc went after her? Apparently, she didn't care. She walked over and stood beside Mara, a look of pride on her face.

"I'm coming, too," said the box seller, closing up the stall. "Business around here is just too slow."

"But . . ." I sputtered. Our mission of going up against Caroc was turning into a parade.

"Don't worry about it," said Irma, seeing my confusion. "They can watch. And maybe the bravest can help Will."

I nodded. Irma was right. These people deserved to see Caroc go down—if we could destroy him.

When we left Hunger, forty or fifty of the town's inhabitants came with us.

"This has to work," I muttered under my breath. "It just *has* to. . . ." I turned my head and looked at Patch, who was riding on my shoulder, a small warm glow of courage and trust.

With so many people following us, we had to change our plan slightly.

"I can't be in two places at once," said Hay Lin. "I'm going to have to try to blow *all* the fumes away in one good blast, so that it will be safe to breathe here while I'm helping out with Caroc. Hold on, everybody!"

The townsfolk looked puzzled at Hay Lin's announcement.

"She can control air," I explained, as if that cleared everything up.

I had barely finished speaking when the first sharp gust of wind came up, followed immediately by another stronger one. In a minute, a full-scale gale was blowing that felt strong enough to knock one or two of the townsfolk off their feet. Luckily, it didn't. The wind howled down the hill toward Caroc, cutting through the poisonous mist and sweeping it aside.

"There," said Hay Lin, letting the wind subside until it was merely a strong but refreshing breeze. "*Now* we can breathe without that stink in our noses."

Of course, while we could now breathe, we had also probably made Caroc aware of our presence. Luckily, that was part of our plan.

"Now it's my turn," Irma said. "I think it's time for a good spring cleaning." Extending her arms, she let blue sparks of power flare out in all directions.

Seconds later, a flood of water came roaring and tumbling down the hillside, rinsing away the nasty gray slime.

"It's safe to walk now," said Irma smugly.

By now, the Hunger people were completely shocked, and Mara had taken on an air of pride.

"I *told* you they weren't just ordinary strangers," she said to the crowd, trying not to look too stunned herself.

Smiling at Mara's words, Will turned to the four of us. "Okay, it's time to start the diversion," she said. "We have to keep Caroc's attention on us, not Cornelia and the others."

"Remember, you only have to get his attention," I said to Mara. "Don't take any chances. And don't get too close to him." I was still feeling anxious because Mara had left Taddy and come with us.

When everyone had gathered, Will started walking down the hill. I noticed that Mara was marching at Will's shoulder with a look of fierce pride on her face. Caroc had definitely made some enemies in Hunger.

"We should get going, too," Taranee said. "There's not much time. And the quicker we are the safer it will be for those people."

Nodding, we agreed and took off. However, we didn't head in the same direction as Will and her little army. They were aiming for Caroc's head, while our goal was his tail.

Would it work? Please, please let it work, I said to myself. We've come too far to fail.

I saw Caroc's head swerve slowly to follow the largest group of people, led by Will. I hoped that he wouldn't notice Taranee, Irma, Hay Lin, or me as we sneaked up to his huge tail.

"Okay, let's stick to the plan. White first," I said, passing one of Mara's jars of paint to Hay Lin. "You know what our art teacher says: it's always important to lay a good foundation."

Just then, we noticed movement near Caroc's head. *Ziiiing!* Will flung her first lightning bolt, and the people of Hunger started yelling and dancing and shouting their heads off, pelting Caroc with rocks from the ground.

"Now," I said tensely, bringing my attention back to the task at hand. "Two big white circles . . ."

"I know," said Hay Lin, and she leaped into the air, clutching the jar of glaze. "Two white circles coming up . . ."

For the moment, Caroc's tail was still, making our job easier. And Mara's paint was much better than regular paint. It was less runny and better at sticking to the rough gray scales that made up the worm's skin.

Suddenly, the great tail heaved and twitched. Hay Lin managed to fly out of the way unharmed. I hoped Will and her brave little army were just as lucky.

"Now blue," I said, handing more paint to Irma.

"Turn back," I heard Will shout. "Turn back!"

A tremor ran through Caroc's body, like a minor earthquake.

"Hurry, hurry, hurry . . ." I yelled. We were running out of time.

"I *am* hurrying!" shouted Irma.

And she was directing the blue paint at her target with amazing speed. Hay Lin swooped down, got the red paint from me, and went in for the finishing touches.

"Run! *Run!*"

It wasn't just Will yelling now. There were many voices, some steady, some panicked. Mara and a few of the others came charging by, and I felt a brief surge of thankfulness that they had kept their heads and were running in the right direction, drawing Caroc after them. . . . But where was Will?

And then Caroc's mighty head came swinging around, his jaw open and fangs gleaming. He was heading straight for us. And although it was exactly what I wanted to have happen, I still had a moment of absolute terror.

I snapped out of my panic attack, put my hand on the earth, and shoved. Next to me, Caroc's tail rose into the air, propelled by the shove I had given the ground. Suddenly, Caroc found himself facing a pair of glaring eyes, a big red mouth, and a spout of flame like something that might come from a dragon. The fact that our dragon's glare had come out slightly cross-eyed was something I hoped Caroc wouldn't notice.

Caroc paused for just a moment. Then he drew back, opened his jaw even wider, and bit down—on his own tail!

"When do you think he's going to realize what he's done?" Irma asked.

"Any minute now," I replied, my stare firmly glued to the giant worm in front of me.

There was a huge choking cough, and the earth trembled. Scales bulged and stretched as he tried to draw back. But Mara was right—once he had taken hold of something, he couldn't let go. Not even when it turned out he was swallowing his own tail.

"Where's Will?" I asked Mara. I was still worried about Will. She should have been with Mara, leading Caroc back to us.

"I don't know," Mara said sadly.

Oh, no! She hadn't been hurt, had she? She couldn't have been. I felt as if I would have known if something bad had happened to her.

"Will!" I yelled frantically. "Will, where are you?" I began running toward where Caroc's head had previously been.

The ground shook as the worm heaved and retched, trying to spit out his tail. I stumbled and moved on, still searching desperately.

Then I saw her.

She lay huddled on the ground, curled up on her side. My heart nearly stopped, but then I noticed she was moving, and I let out a big sigh of relief.

"Will!" I cried.

"I'm here." Will sounded weak and out of breath. I wondered if Caroc had hurt her.

"Are you all right?" I asked when I reached her side.

"I'm fine," Will said. "I just need to . . . catch my . . . breath."

"What happened to you?" I asked when she had managed to recover.

A small grin spread across her face. "I got knocked down by my own army. Accidentally, of course . . ."

She pushed herself off the ground and sat there for a moment, watching Caroc as he struggled. "I'm okay," she said, and patted my hand reassuringly. "You should finish your plan."

"Yes," I answered. "It's time for some earth magic."

Though more than one element had suffered, it was earth that had been the most damaged by Caroc's greed. Healing this earth was a huge task, and considering how hard it had been to grow a single small peach, I didn't know if I could do it. I had no idea where I would get the strength.

Help.

I smiled. Patch had returned and was hovering in front of me. "Thanks, Patch. I know you'll help," I said. His sturdy loyalty was a small spot of warmth, but he was just one little green spark, and Caroc was a giant monster.

Many help. Far away and close by.

Far away? Maybe Patch meant that the green sparks had fled to Heatherfield. But close by? I had not seen any hint of green apart from Patch.

It was at that moment that I felt a horrible sensation of being swallowed and trapped.

Suddenly, I understood where Patch's kin were—they were *inside* the worm.

My first instinct was to get something sharp and cut him open. But then I realized that that wouldn't solve anything. Patch was not a real, physical body, and it wasn't in the colossal belly of the worm that I should look for those sparks Caroc had swallowed. Rather, it was in the darkness of his greedy soul.

I shuddered at the thought.

"Will," I said softly. "I think I'm going to need a little help."

I didn't have to say any more. She understood, and brought out the Heart. I looked at its gentle light for a very long time, taking it in, making sure I carried the memory and glow of the Heart inside me. I was afraid that where I was going, even the memory of light would be hard to hold on to. Bracing myself, I stood up.

Slowly, I began making my way across the broken ground that still shook as Caroc bucked and heaved. Even though I knew he couldn't physically hurt me, I felt a shiver of fear slide down my spine. When I was near enough to look straight into his vast, mud-colored eyes, I stopped. For a moment, he grew still. He watched me with cold fury. There was no doubt he would have lunged at me if he could have.

Suppressing a shudder, I reached out and placed one hand on his scaly skin. The scales were not smooth, as I had thought they would be. They were rough, like sharkskin. They were the scales of a true monster.

As soon as I touched him, I felt it. Fear and darkness. Darkness and greed. I didn't want to go there, but I had no choice.

I closed my eyes and let the nightmare take me in.

There are all kinds of darkness. But none of them are like the darkness inside the worm.

It was a darkness without hope, an endless misery that swallowed up all joy, all strength, all life.

And I was in it.

I was looking for something, but I couldn't

remember what. But it didn't matter, anyway. In this place, I knew that nothing lost was ever found. How could you look for something in a place where it was so dark you might as well have been blind? Hopelessness swamped me. I could *feel* the darkness eating away at me, sapping my strength and my hope.

"You won't last long."

A cold voice rang out. Somehow, I knew who the voice belonged to. It was Caroc.

"Oh, really? You think so?" I said, with automatic defiance. But I didn't believe my words. I knew he was right.

"Pretty little girl. So used to sunlight and praise and easy victories. Well, not this time, little girl. This time, I win."

A small anger stirred inside me.

"You're just a big worm. And at the moment, you're busy swallowing your own tail. Where's the victory in that?" I said, with more courage than I thought I had.

Cold fury pounded me, trying to force me to be silent, trying to destroy me.

"I have you, don't I? You came here. And here, I don't need a mouth to swallow you. I have hold of you, and I'm not letting go. You won't last long. You won't *want* to last." Caroc made a noise almost like a laugh, but there was no joy in it, just evil.

My small flame of anger died. He was right. Trapped in this cold, dark misery, why would I want to last? There was no hope here. No hope at all. Why had I even come?

And then, impossibly, a tiny glow appeared in the vast, unending darkness. A small, green glow.

Patch.

Patch had followed me into the darkness of the worm. His small light trembled with weariness and fear, and I wondered if he would survive. But he was there, and in his glow there was an echo of a greater light, a greater strength. In his glow, I felt strength. Suddenly, I remembered the Heart.

"Help me," I whispered. "Help me now."

All at once, I knew I was not alone. I knew I was not weak. I knew that somewhere there was sunlight, and friendship, and a reason to fight this darkness.

"Sorry, Caroc," I said boldly. "But I think you just lost your battle."

Remembering sunlight, remembering greenness and growing things, I spread my arms wide and called to them. Out of the darkness, green sparks came flocking, in twos and threes, then dozens, then a whole joyous whirl. It was a flood of green sparks.

I felt the darkness draw back, shrinking, until it was nearly nothing. I opened my eyes and gasped.

I was standing in the middle of a whirling, sparkling blizzard of green. There was so much green that, for a moment, I could see nothing else.

Wild joy rose in me, and I laughed happily. Caroc had been destroyed. We were free.

A moment later, I felt a wave of gratitude that told me just how thankful the green sparks were. It felt like being engulfed in a giant, green hug.

"Go," I urged them gently. "Go heal this land."

They took off, soaring.

As the sparks flew, new grass spread over the barren hills like a huge carpet being unrolled. Dead stumps exploded into leafy greenness. Withered blueberry bushes went from bare twigs to leaves and flowers and then berries as we watched.

"Oh," said Mara softly. "Oh." Tears of joy and wonder streaked down her thin face. "I suppose we'll have to change the name of the town again. Seems we'll be living in Plenty once more."

There was very little left of Caroc. Around the castle walls where he had lain, there was now a dark, muddy moat. At the bottom of the moat, a very thin worm wriggled around, still trying to eat his own tail.

With a creaking sound of long-unused gears, the castle finally lowered its drawbridge, and the first person to walk across it was Prince Florian himself.

He was the perfect fairy-tale prince, with sleek blond hair, piercing blue eyes, and a face that was handsome, if a little thin.

"A joyous day," he said. "A joyous, joyous day. Whom can I thank for this deliverance?"

Suddenly, everyone was looking at me. Everyone, including the handsome Prince Florian.

8

Who knew that saving the town of Plenty would have been an excuse for a party? But it was, and the townspeople were going crazy getting ready. My friends and I had been ushered into a beautiful room and told to wait. We didn't have to wait long.

"Prince Florian sent you these," said an elegant, gray-haired lady. She was the prince's royal mother, Queen Flora. In her wake came five ladies-in-waiting, each carrying a glittering gown. "And perhaps you'll permit my maids to help you with your hair?"

"Er . . . ah . . . yes." I said, even though what I wanted most just then was a good, hot shower. Luckily, baths were on the agenda, too—warm baths that were scented with petals from the roses that once again covered the castle walls.

After the baths came a styling session that made the preparations for Mr. Sacharino's photo shoot look like nothing special. We were primped, moussed, powdered, and pampered. We all got special treatment.

Then came the gowns.

Pink for Will, lavender for Hay Lin, deep blue for Irma, and for Taranee a gorgeous, flaming scarlet.

But I have to admit I loved mine the most. It was white, with touches of green emeralds stitched to the hem and neckline. As I whirled back and forth in front of the mirror, it occurred to me that the white dress looked suspiciously like a bridal gown. What was going on here? I wondered.

"Prince Florian sent this?" I asked the lady-in-waiting who had helped me into it.

"Oh, well, actually," the woman said, "Her Majesty, Queen Flora, did. But I am sure the prince approves."

Oh, he does, does he? I thought. Before I could say another word, a new lady-in-waiting appeared holding a box.

Inside was a pair of shoes.

"These," I said, horrified, "are made of glass!"

Things were getting a little out of hand. I was

beginning to fear that I had entered a real fairy tale. But there was no way of avoiding the situation, so I put them on. They were extremely comfortable. And, surprise, surprise . . . a perfect fit.

"Will," I said. "Do you notice anything strange going on? Other than what we've done, I mean."

"No, not really," she said. "Why?"

"Oh, I don't know." I said. "This gown, these glass slippers . . ."

"You look beautiful," she said.

"Thanks," I muttered miserably.

My misery only increased later, when the music started up and Prince Florian approached me and asked, with perfect manners, if I would care to begin the ball with him. I was, after all, his guest of honor, he pointed out.

There was no way I could say no. He was just being polite and thanking me for destroying Caroc. At least, that's what I told myself as he swung me onto the dance floor. Of course, he was a very good dancer, and I did feel like a princess as the whole court looked on with approving smiles. This, they must have thought, looking at the two of us, was how the story ought to end. I, on the other hand, wasn't so sure.

After what seemed like an endless number of

dances, the handsome prince led me away from the crowded ballroom and out into the blooming rose garden.

"So . . . uh . . . are you comfortable?" he asked awkwardly. The elegant assurance he had shown on the dance floor had vanished. Now he seemed just like any normal, nervous guy. "You aren't too cold or anything? I could get you a shawl. Or maybe you would like something warm to eat," he said earnestly.

"I'm fine," I replied.

"It's just . . . you see . . ." he stumbled and stuttered, trying to get his words out. "I have something to tell you."

"Actually, I have something to tell you, too," I said.

"Oh?" He looked surprised. Probably the usual script for this sort of thing did not call for the girl to say anything except, "I will."

There was an awkward silence.

"This is highly embarrassing," Prince Florian finally said. "I'm going to have to tell you that I haven't fallen in love with you."

"Oh, *good*," I said, relief flooding through me. "I mean, not that it wouldn't have been very nice, but . . ."

He smiled. "Yes, but . . ."

"It just seemed to be what everyone expected," I told him. "The gown, the glass slippers. All of it. . . ."

"I know. But you're not . . . you're really not the least bit in love with me?" He looked at me anxiously. "Because I certainly don't want to hurt your feelings."

I laughed. "No. I'm not the least bit in love," I said firmly.

At least, not with you, I added silently, thinking of Caleb. One fairy-tale hero was enough for me.

"Good. I'm so glad to hear that. Because, you see, I have Anna."

"Anna?" I thought of the numerous gowned beauties in the ballroom and couldn't help feeling a small stab of curiosity. I wanted to know who had caught the prince's heart. "Who is she?" I asked.

"The dessert cook," he explained. "Or at least, that's what she was while there was still anything left to make desserts with. Later, she became the reason I stayed alive."

Well, well, I thought. Prince Florian was a boy full of surprises. There clearly was a romantic and unconventional heart under the elegant clothes.

For a moment, I was tempted to stick around to see what happened when he announced the engagement. I didn't think Her Majesty, Queen Flora, would be very happy, and some of his courtiers would be shocked and disapproving. But I was pretty sure the people of Plenty would approve.

"Congratulations," I said, smiling. "And good luck."

He beamed back at me. "Thank you. Perhaps, when we have children, you'd like to be a fairy godmother instead?"

I smiled back, still lightheaded with relief. "I'll think about it."

Somewhere, the castle clock had begun to strike. Twelve times, I was sure. I kicked off the glass slippers.

"Here," I said, and handed them to the prince. "Give them to Anna. I'm sure they'll fit her perfectly!"

It was time for this princess to head home. The fairy tale was over.

⊜ ⊜ ⊜ ⊚ ⊜

It was much harder to say good-bye to Patch. I wanted to hug him, but since I couldn't, I just sent him a wave of love.

The Oracle, when he sent us back to Heatherfield, had some consoling words for me.

"He chose to be your friend, Guardian. And

true friends are not meant to be kept apart forever. I'm sure you will see him again."

"Can he . . . visit sometimes?" I asked.

"Quite possibly. Spirits such as Patch are not bound by the same laws of time and space as human beings, which is why he and his kin were able to come to you in the first place. They knew that you would help. Their effort was extreme, but they needed to get your attention. Patch, as you call him, and the others were drawn to you because of your power over earth. He is an unusually brave and stubborn spirit, is he not?"

"Yes," I said, and I couldn't help smiling. "He certainly is."

With that, the Oracle sent us home, adjusting time and space so it was as if we had left Heatherfield for only a second.

The surprises weren't quite over. A few weeks later I had a surprise visitor. No, it wasn't Patch, but someone much more surprising. When the doorbell rang, I opened the door to find Acey Jones in the hall, clutching a briefcase.

"Hello, Cornelia," he said, with a brilliant smile. "May I come in?"

"I guess so," I said a little coldly. I was not about to be fooled by his smile again.

"I assume you have seen this," he said,

fishing a magazine from the briefcase. When he pulled his hand out, he was holding the latest issue of *Red Hot*.

He handed the magazine to me, and I let out a little shriek of surprise. On the cover, looking beautiful and larger than life, was my face, framed by the hood of the Little Red Riding Hood cloak. Brilliant green streaks highlighted my hair and made me sparkle. One of them was probably Patch, I thought with a smile.

The tagline read, THIS GIRL IS MAGIC.

Lilian, who had just bound into the room, snatched the magazine out of my hands. "Let me see, let me see," she chanted. "I want to see it, too!"

"So, *Red Hot* absolutely adored your pictures," Acey said. "And Mr. Sacharino is enormously pleased. So pleased, in fact, that he is offering you a fantastic opportunity!"

He stood there, smiling, waiting for me to ask him what the fantastic opportunity was. To fall at his feet in gratitude.

I didn't.

His smile stiffened slightly. "His new autumn line is a *brilliant* creation called Space Angels," he explained. "And he'd like you to model it!"

"Really?" I said. "But I thought you fired me."

"Cornelia, that was . . . that was just a friendly misunderstanding," Acey cooed smoothly. "You know how this business is. You would make a stunning Space Angel!"

His smile grew bright once more, and, for a moment, looked almost warm. But it was all on the surface. I knew he didn't really like me and that the only reason he was there was because his boss had sent him. I knew he was no monster, but, as I watched him smile that brilliant but fake smile, I couldn't help seeing a touch of the cold greed of Caroc. And I had had enough greed to last me a lifetime.

"No thanks," I said calmly. "I'm afraid I can't help you."

He was shocked. He clearly wasn't used to being turned down.

"Oh. Well, I . . . Mr. Sacharino will be very disappointed," Acey sniffed.

"I'm sorry," I repeated, even though we both knew I wasn't.

When he showed no signs of leaving, I held out my hand. "Good-bye, Mr. Jones," I said.

"Acey. Call me Acey." He looked at me incredulously. "Are you *sure* . . ."

"Quite sure," I replied, and, ushering him out, closed the door.

I looked down at Lilian, who was at my side. "Lilian, would you like to play a game?" I asked. "Or go see a movie?"

She stared at me for a moment, disbelief in her blue eyes. Then she turned and ran from the room, screaming.

"Mom, Mom," she wailed. "Help! Cornelia is being *nice* to me!"

I laughed. It was good to be back where there was plenty of light, hope, and . . . love.